Animals Helping to Detect Diseases

SUSAN H. GRAY

Children's Press®
An Imprint of Scholastic Inc.
New York Toronto London Auckland Sydney
Mexico City New Delhi Hong Kong
Danbury, Connecticut

Content Consultant
Dr. Stephen S. Ditchkoff
Professor of Wildlife Sciences
Auburn University
Auburn, Alabama

Library of Congress Cataloging-in-Publication Data
Gray, Susan Heinrichs, author.
  Animals helping to detect diseases / Author, Susan H. Gray.
     pages cm. — (A true book)
  Summary: "Learn how animals can be trained to detect diseases in humans."— Provided by
publisher.
  Audience: Ages 9–12.
  Audience: Grades 4 to 6.
  Includes bibliographical references and index.
  ISBN 978-0-531-21214-1 (library binding : alk. paper) — ISBN 978-0-531-21288-2 (pbk. : alk. paper)
1. Detector dogs—Juvenile literature. 2. Medicine, Preventive—Juvenile literature. 3. Animal train-
ing—Juvenile literature. 4. Working dogs—Juvenile literature. I. Title. II. Series: True book.
  RA436.G73 2015
  636.088'6—dc23   2014030586

© 2015 Scholastic Inc.
All rights reserved. Published in 2015 by Children's Press, an imprint of Scholastic Inc. Published
simultaneously in Canada. Printed in China 62
SCHOLASTIC, CHILDREN'S PRESS, A TRUE BOOK™, and associated logos are trademarks and/or
registered trademarks of Scholastic Inc.
1 2 3 4 5 6 7 8 9 10 R 24 23 22 21 20 19 18 17 16 15

**Front cover: A medical detection dog
checking samples for cancer**

**Back cover: An African giant pouched
rat sniffing samples for tuberculosis**

Find the Truth!

Everything you are about to read is true *except* for one of the sentences on this page.

Which one is **TRUE**?

T or F Rats, mice, and fruit flies are being used to detect diseases.

T or F A dog's nose is about as sensitive to odors as a human's nose.

Find the answers in this book.

Contents

THE **BIG** TRUTH!

Inside a Dog's Nose

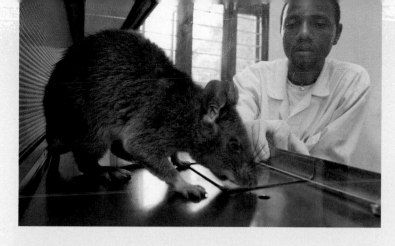

An African giant pouched rat sniffs for disease.

Fruit flies have been used to study diseases in space.

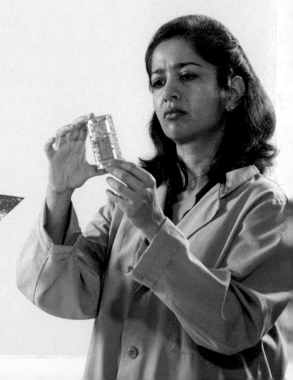

5

A dog sniffs at a suspicious sample while learning to detect cancer.

CHAPTER 1

Disease Detectives

In Mexico, a doctor is figuring out why a child is dizzy. In India, a lab worker peers at a **vial** of blood. In Florida, a golden retriever sniffs at a jar with fluid in it. In Africa, a rat inhales from a container of air. What is happening in each of these situations? A medical worker is identifying a disease.

In the United States, there are about five doctors for every 2,000 people.

Not Without Problems

To **diagnose** a patient, doctors might order x-rays or blood tests. Sometimes, it takes days to get the results. Often, the tests are very expensive. Therefore, scientists are looking for better ways to make diagnoses.

In some countries, this is especially important. Hospitals are rare. Patients are very unwell by the time they arrive. They need quick diagnoses.

A doctor can learn a lot about a patient's health from a sample of the patient's blood.

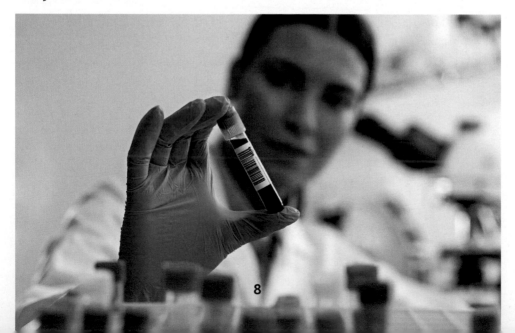

A medic works with a newborn baby in a displaced community in Southeast Asia.

In some countries, five doctors are serving more than 100,000 people.

Often, hospitals in these areas have little money. The newest equipment may not be available. The hospital could be low on testing supplies. There may not be a laboratory nearby. It could take a long time to get test results back. Experts have tried for years to solve these problems. It turns out that some answers were right under their noses.

Hippocrates
is often called
the father of
medicine.

CHAPTER 2

Things Come Together

The science of diagnosis goes back many centuries. Egyptian physician Imhotep diagnosed and treated patients more than 4,600 years ago. Hippocrates, another famous physician, did the same in Greece about 2,400 years ago.

In the 1800s, William Farr of Great Britain became interested in identifying diseases. At the time, doctors did not know exactly why their patients died. Diseases went by many different names and nicknames. This was very confusing.

William Farr's work still impacts medicine today.

Documenting Diseases

Farr wanted medicine to be better organized. He wanted diagnoses to be more orderly. With this in mind, he gathered information from other doctors. Then he made a list of diseases. The list included a description of each illness and the **symptoms** that patients had. Doctors originally used this to identify a person's cause of death. However, this could also be used to diagnose living people.

This idea caught on. Over time, many people added to the knowledge of illnesses. Today, we know about thousands of diseases. We now have specific, standard names for them. For many diseases, we know the causes. Doctors are much better at identifying diseases. Nurses know how they affect patients. Disease detection is not perfect, but it is much more organized.

Diseases used to have names like quinsy and jail fever.

Two medics check on a sick patient.

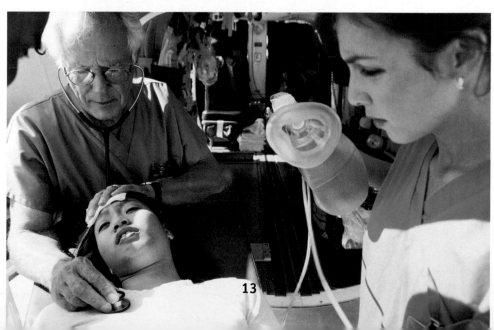

13

Meanwhile . . .

As medicine was advancing, other fields were, too. People were learning more about animals. They discovered that certain animals had amazing talents. They began putting those talented animals to work.

In England, the police worked with dogs. They saw how dogs could follow scents, so they began using bloodhounds to track down thieves. These dogs helped solve crimes.

Bloodhounds were used in the historic search for Jack the Ripper in London, England, in the late 19th century.

Hunters used bloodhounds more than 800 years ago.

14

The Saint Bernard gets its name from the mountain pass between Italy and Switzerland where it became famous for rescuing lost travelers.

In Switzerland, **monks** were putting Saint Bernard dogs to work. At first, these large dogs pulled carts. Some also guarded property. But then the monks noticed something. The dogs were not just strong. They also had a great sense of smell. They could find their way home in the snow and could locate travelers who were lost in the mountains. The monks began using Saint Bernards as rescue dogs.

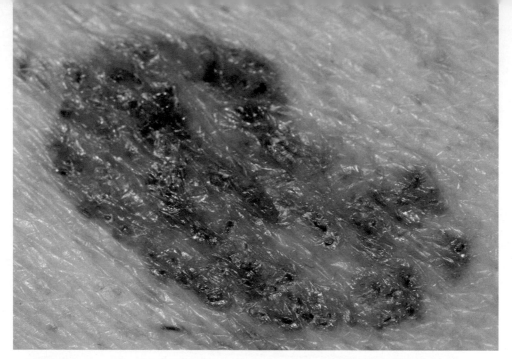

Skin cancer is the most common form of cancer in the United States.

Discovering Other Talents

In the 20th century, Hywel Williams was treating patients in England. He was especially interested in skin diseases. One day, he had a patient with a spot of skin cancer. The patient told Williams an interesting story. Her dog was constantly sniffing the spot. This made her decide to come in for a checkup. The story got Williams thinking. Could dogs detect skin cancer?

Super Smellers

Belgian Bart Weetjens had always liked rats. He knew they were smart and could be trained. He also knew they had an acute sense of smell. At first, he wanted to teach rats to find explosives in old battlefields. Weetjens began his work in 1997. In time, his rats were doing a great job. Then he had another idea. Perhaps rats could detect diseases such as **tuberculosis** (TB), a dangerous lung disease. Again, he was correct! Now, his TB-detecting rats are at work in Africa.

A dog might be trained to lie down or sit down when it smells cancer cells.

CHAPTER 3

Doctor Dogs

Hywel Williams thought a lot about his patient's dog. He knew that dogs have a good sense of smell. Perhaps any dog could sniff out skin cancer.

In time, more doctors became interested in this idea. They began testing dogs. They wanted to see if dogs could find other types of cancer, too. With every new test, the dogs proved they could. They sniffed out lung, skin, bladder, and other cancers.

The moisture on a dog's nose helps capture odors in the air.

What's Going On?

What exactly do the dogs smell? They probably smell **volatile organic compounds**, known as VOCs. Volatile materials evaporate quickly. Organic compounds contain carbon and other atoms.

When VOCs evaporate, their molecules disperse into the air. People cannot smell very small amounts of VOCs, but dogs can. Williams's patient with skin cancer was very lucky. Her dog smelled VOCs on her skin and would not leave her alone.

A dog's sensitive nose can pick up scents a human never notices.

20

A lot of the VOCs in the air come from plants.

Many VOCs have a strong smell. Gasoline, for example, is a VOC. Fingernail polish remover is also one. The smells of a new car are probably from VOCs.

Those are man-made compounds. But VOCs also exist in nature. Plants give off plenty of them, but most people do not notice. Animals give them off, too. Diseased tissues also release VOCs. These natural VOCs are the ones that dogs detect so well.

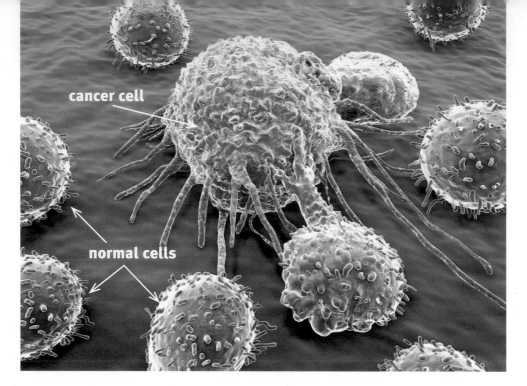

cancer cell

normal cells

Because cancer cells are so different from normal cells, they have a different smell.

Cancer cells act differently than normal cells. Cancer cells multiply rapidly and **emit** particular VOCs. The VOCs might show up in a patient's breath. They might be present around a spot on the skin. They might even appear in a patient's urine. Perhaps they are in sweat, earwax, and tears. There are all sorts of places where VOCs might show up.

Dogs on Duty

Today, dogs are used to detect lung and breast cancer. They do this simply by smelling a patient's breath. They are trained to sit or lie down when they sense cancer VOCs. Dogs can also detect bladder cancer. To do this, they sniff just a tiny bit of a patient's urine.

Dogs are amazingly good at this. They are very accurate and quite fast. They also work cheaply!

Dogs that detect diseases are called medical detection dogs.

The dog will sit by the sample that she detects has cancer.

Other Illnesses

Dogs can do more than detect cancer. They can tell when a patient is low on sugar. They also know when someone is about to have a **seizure**. In these cases, they might smell VOCs, but they also might notice other things. Perhaps they see that someone is getting shaky. Maybe they hear changes in a person's voice. They alert people by nudging them or by barking.

Service dogs such as seizure alert dogs form close relationships with their humans.

Medical detection dogs start their training at only 8 weeks old.

Dogs in England are being trained to find bedbugs.

Dogs have yet another talent. They can smell germs. Hospitals always try to keep germs under control, but some germs are very tough to get rid of.

Dogs can smell germs in the air and can tell which patients are carrying them. These dogs are very helpful. They show nurses which patients need more care. They can also show which rooms need a good cleaning.

Inside a Dog's Nose

What makes dog noses so special? Why can dogs smell things that people cannot? One reason is that dogs have more cells that detect scents. Humans have only 5 million or 6 million of these cells. Dogs have between 200 million and 300 million! Also, our brains are different. Everyone has a brain area that analyzes smells. However, in dogs, this section makes up a larger portion of the brain than it does in humans.

Dog and human nostrils are different, too. We cannot wiggle our nostrils the way dogs wiggle theirs. Dogs can turn their nostrils sideways one at a time. In doing this, the nose picks up smells from two different directions. That helps the dog know where odors are coming from.

Scientists are trying to learn more about dog noses. They hope to understand how a dog's nose can detect disease.

CHAPTER 4

Other Animals Get Involved

Dogs are not the only animals with medical jobs. Rats, mice, and flies are hard at work, too. Rats can sniff out the germ that causes tuberculosis, or TB. TB is very common in some African countries. The rats being used to detect it are also very common in Africa. But these are no ordinary rats. They are African giant pouched rats.

It takes between 6 to 12 months of training for the African giant pouched rats to learn how to detect TB.

A rat walks along a line of samples, sniffing for evidence of TB.

The rats' reward usually contains mashed bananas.

What the Rats Do

This is how rats do their work. First, they must be trained. In training, rats smell two different kinds of samples: fluids with the TB germs, and fluids without. The rats scratch around a sample each time they smell the germ. When they are correct, they get a reward. Only the best rats go on to work in hospitals as disease detectors.

At the hospital, they work in a lab. Doctors collect fluid from their patients' lungs. The fluid goes into little containers. Next, a trained rat is brought in. The rat sniffs the containers. After sniffing each container, the rat either scratches or moves on. Lab workers note which containers made the rats scratch. This way, doctors know which patients have TB.

An African giant pouched rat gets its name from the pouches in its cheeks.

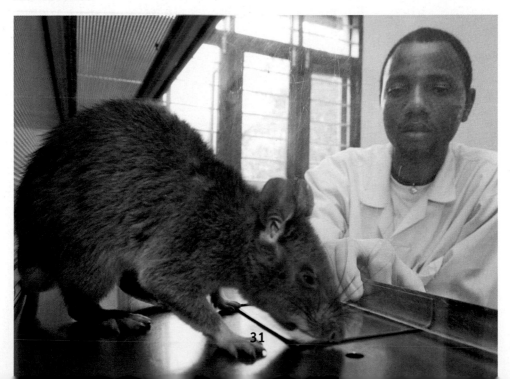

Without rats, lab workers find TB by dyeing fluid samples and looking at them under a microscope. This process is slow and not very accurate. There must be many TB germs present or lab workers will miss them. In addition, areas of Africa have few hospitals. They may be short on lab workers or equipment. African giant rats take only a few seconds to find TB germs without dye or microscopes.

Heating a glass slide containing a fluid sample helps highlight any evidence of TB.

Rats in Action

African pouched rats have found quite a bit of success in Africa. Since 2008, the rats have screened more than 200,000 samples in Dar es Salaam, Tanzania. They found about 5,000 TB cases that human screeners missed. In Maputo, Mozambique, the rats have been in use since 2013. In their first year, they found an extra 556 TB cases in the nearly 20,000 samples they screened.

Avian flu could potentially destroy a chicken farm.

The first known case of a person getting avian flu was in 1997.

Sniffing Out Avian Flu

Mice are catching up with dogs and rats. Mice can identify birds with **avian** flu. This is a disease that spreads from bird to bird. The flu can kill chickens, turkeys, and pet birds. It can spread through chicken farms, destroying their chicken populations. It can also infect people, making them sick.

Mice can identify infected birds by their droppings. No one knows exactly what the mice smell. It is probably VOCs. But trained mice can become quite good at this.

Mice could someday be on the front lines against this disease. They might be able to sniff out the first sick duck in a city park. They might find the one infected bird at the zoo. This could keep the disease from spreading.

Mice, like many animals, have a very good sense of smell.

The Smallest Workers

Fruit flies are tiny—not much bigger than pinheads. However, they detect diseases just like dogs and rats do. Like these other animals, fruit flies detect VOCs.

Fruit flies do not have noses, but they can still smell things. They use their **antennae**. These organs pick up odors in the air. This helps the fly find fruit. And that's not all. Different odors cause the antennae to change colors.

A microscope is needed for a good look at a fruit fly and its antennae.

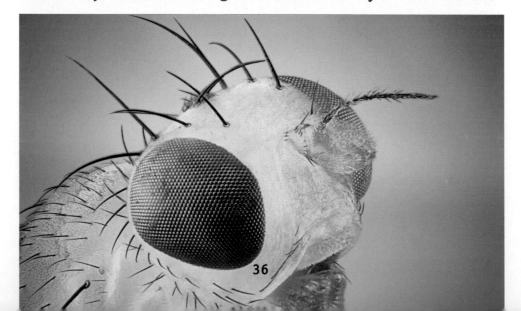

36

Ripe fruits emit VOCs.

A group of scientists wanted to study these flies. They wondered about the flies' sense of smell. Could the flies smell VOCs in cancer cells? If so, would their antennae change color? How could someone see those colors? After all, it is hard to see anything on these tiny flies. The scientists thought a long time. How could they answer these questions?

The scientists decided to use a microscope with a special light on it. They put the fruit flies under the microscope. The light made their antennae colors show up really well.

Next, the scientists blew air over the flies. Some was air that had been around cancer cells. Some was air that had been around normal cells.

Timeline of Medical Diagnosis

About 430 B.C.E.
Hippocrates works as a doctor in Greece.

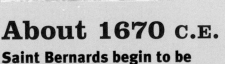

About 1670 C.E.
Saint Bernards begin to be used in rescue work in the Alps.

The scientists watched closely. They saw the antennae change colors. Antennae had one color pattern in the normal air. They had another pattern in the air exposed to cancer.

The flies could show the difference! They did not have to be trained. No one had to give them rewards. Their antennae colors changed automatically. The scientists were excited. Flies had detected VOCs from cancer cells.

1830s to 1870s
William Farr improves descriptions of diseases.

2008
Bart Weetjens begins using rats to detect tuberculosis.

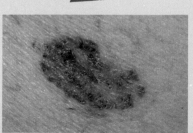

1989
Hywel Williams publishes an article about a cancer patient's dog.

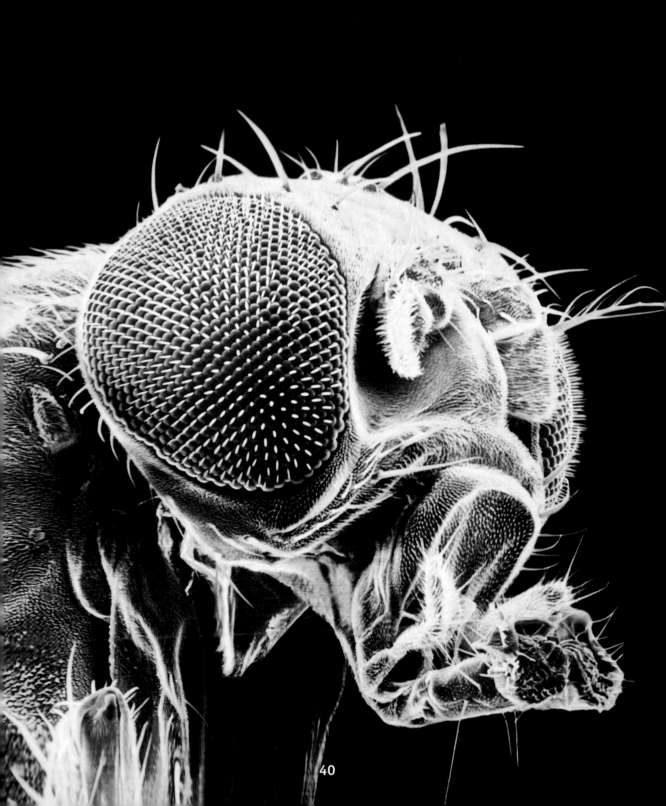

CHAPTER 5

Coming Soon

Scientists are looking at more ways to use dogs, rats, and mice. One day, these animals might be used to detect many types of cancer. Maybe they will be finding other diseases.

Fruit flies are also getting more attention. Some experts think they can grow "smarter" flies. Maybe these flies will even glow when they come near cancer cells.

Fruit flies are cheap and easy to keep in a lab.

An e-nose was sent into space on the International Space Station for several months to study the spacecraft's air supply.

New Detectors

Scientists are also testing bees. These insects learn quickly. They can learn to respond to certain smells. Perhaps they can be put to use detecting VOCs.

Some experts are creating "electronic noses." These machines are able to sense tiny amounts of VOCs. Some e-noses have already been built. They analyze the gases in a patient's breath and can detect lung cancer.

It is possible that many labs will use e-noses someday. However, e-noses might be too expensive for some hospitals. There may also be problems shipping them to some countries.

On the other hand, rats, mice, and dogs are everywhere. They are very accurate in their medical work. They work for small rewards. Because of this, animals will continue to be used to detect diseases for years to come. ★

Some scientists say that dogs are still more accurate than current e-noses.

Number of deadly diseases on William Farr's list: 27

Number of lives saved by Saint Bernard dogs in the Alps: About 2,000

Number of new cases of TB in the world in 2012: 8.6 million

Biggest producers of VOCs: Plants

Biggest source of man-made VOCs: The transportation industry

Time it takes a dog to sniff out germs in a hospital ward: About 10 minutes

African countries using rats to find TB: Tanzania and Mozambique

Did you find the truth?

Rats, mice, and fruit flies are being used to detect diseases.

A dog's nose is about as sensitive to odors as a human's nose.

Resources

Books

Goldish, Meish. *Dogs*. New York: Bearport Publishing, 2007.

Ruffin, Frances. *Medical Detective Dogs*. New York: Bearport Publishing, 2006.

Visit this Scholastic Web site for more information on animals helping to detect diseases:

★ www.factsfornow.scholastic.com
Enter the keywords **Animals Helping to Detect Diseases**

Important Words

antennae (an-TEN-ee) — feelers on the head of an insect

avian (AY-vee-uhn) — relating to birds

diagnose (dye-uhg-NOHS) — to determine what disease a patient has or what the cause of a problem is

emit (i-MIT) — to produce or send out something such as heat, light, signals, or sound

monks (MUHNGKS) — men who live apart from society in a religious community according to strict rules

seizure (SEE-zhur) — a sudden attack or spasm

symptoms (SIMP-tuhmz) — signs of an illness

tuberculosis (too-bur-kyuh-LOH-sis) — a highly contagious disease caused by bacteria that usually affects the lungs

vial (VYE-uhl) — a very small glass or plastic container

volatile organic compounds (VAH-luh-tile or-GAN-ik KAHM-powndz) — chemicals that evaporate quickly into the air

Index

Page numbers in **bold** indicate illustrations.

About the Author

Susan H. Gray has a master's degree in zoology and has written more than 140 reference books for children. She especially likes to write about animals and on topics that engage children in science. She and her husband, Michael, live in Cabot, Arkansas.

THE JOY OF
A PEANUTS CHRISTMAS
50 Years of Holiday Comics!

Hallmark
BOOKS

CONTENTS

INTRODUCTION

Charles Schulz is the cartoon champion of all time...
He is a magician with a pencil.

—JOYCE C. HALL, FOUNDER, HALLMARK CARDS, INC.

In some way, we can all relate to the trials and tribulations,
the fun and foibles of the PEANUTS gang.

—DONALD J. HALL, CHAIRMAN, HALLMARK CARDS, INC., AND SON OF JOYCE C. HALL

PEANUTS and Hallmark have been playing on the same team for more than forty years, but unlike the ill-fated baseball team Charlie Brown valiantly captains, ours has always been a winning combination. Together we've created over one hundred different products—cards, ornaments, address books, yo-yos and even a Hallmark Hall of Fame production. Together we've shared in the joys and sorrows, the laughter and loves of the whole PEANUTS gang: Charlie Brown and Snoopy, Lucy and Linus, Sally and Schroeder, Peppermint Patty and Marcie, Franklin and Pig-Pen, Woodstock and Spike. We've seen them grow up (sort of), fall in and out of love (in a manner of speaking) and set off on adventures and journeys from Snoopy's Red Baron flights to Linus's relentless quest for the Great Pumpkin.

And we're proud to have been a part of it all.

For us, it all began on May 16, 1960, when Charles Schulz agreed to create four greeting cards for our company. Forty years and more than one hundred products later, the Schulz family and my own have become both great business partners and great friends. Sparky and I shared a love of golf, and, like Charlie Brown, we always hoped that the next game would be better.

I think PEANUTS and Hallmark get along so well because we have so much in common. We're both known for a dedication to quality. We share a commitment to family and community. And we both bring good feelings—warmth, joy, happiness and love—into the daily lives of millions. We're a perfect match. "They think a lot of times of things I wish I had thought of myself," Charles Schulz once said of our family business. "I frequently look at their cards and think, 'I wish I'd used that in my strip.'" Believe me, the feeling is mutual.

A cartoon strip, after all, tells a story—much like a card. And one of the truly magical things about PEANUTS is the way that the characters so truthfully share their emotions. Maybe that's why they work so well in greeting cards.

We've learned a lot of things about Charles Schulz and his PEANUTS gang over the years. We've learned that all PEANUTS characters are right-handed (one of our artists accidentally drew Peppermint Patty writing with her left hand). We learned that Schroeder only listens to

Beethoven (one of our designers once mistakenly drew rows and rows of music by a different composer). We learned that despite their cartoony nature, each PEANUTS character actually has a human hand (another designer once drew a character with only three fingers and a thumb).

But mostly, we've learned what millions of people around the world already know about PEANUTS—that it simply, honestly and beautifully teaches us about life. After all, despite all the gang's quarrels, trials and tribulations, they always come together when it's really important.

When Charles Schulz died in February of 2000, the world lost more than a brilliant artist, a creator of cultural icons and a national treasure. We lost a man who loved his work, who loved his family, who loved his country. We lost a man who spoke his message clearly through his beloved characters and taught us that we can all win the game if we work together, if we love, if we laugh and if we keep on trying.

Somehow, it doesn't matter that Charlie Brown never did kick that football. That he kept trying was enough.

I hope you enjoy this look back at the PEANUTS gang over the years—from the '50s through the '90s. We at Hallmark are delighted to be publishing this one-of-a-kind collection of Charles Schulz's classic Christmas strips, in honor of *The Joy of a PEANUTS Christmas*.

—DON HALL

THE '50s

December 24, 1951

December 15, 1952

January 12, 1953

December 18, 1958

February 22, 1953

CHARLIE BROWN
His dog calls him "that round-headed kid" and his friends sometimes call him "blockhead," but everyone knows him by his full name. He is Charlie Brown, the occasionally tarnished star of the gang, a born loser who

"CHRISTMAS EVE IS MY FAVORITE DAY OF THE YEAR. IT MAKES ME FEEL GOOD ABOUT EVERYTHING."

never loses hope. Even though his baseball team always loses, Lucy always pulls the football away, and his friends ridicule his Christmas tree, Charlie Brown keeps trying and always faces the coming holiday or sport season with optimism.

"PEANUTS"

December 25, 1953

December 25, 1954

PIG-PEN

Pig-Pen always wanders around in a cloud—of dirt. And he leaves dirt on everything in his path. But Pig-Pen has accepted his dirtiness and is happy that way. His Christmastime snowmen may not be the cleanest snowmen in town, but at least they've got character—just like Pig-Pen.

January 6, 1955

January 13, 1955

November 21, 1957

December 21, 1959

LUCY

Lucille Van Pelt is crabby, loud, often angry, and proud of it. She makes no attempt to hide her emotions or her opinions and can be just plain mean to her brother Linus, her friends and even the neighborhood dog. She always knows the answers (she's the neighborhood psychiatrist), she's always right (no matter what the facts say), and she is always in charge (whether or not anyone wants her to be). Despite resistance from Schroeder, she continues to pursue him by hanging mistletoe at Christmas or leaning seductively on his piano.

"I JUST NOTICED SOMETHING ABOUT THIS ROOM. THERE'S AN APPALLING LACK OF MISTLETOE."

December 31, 1956

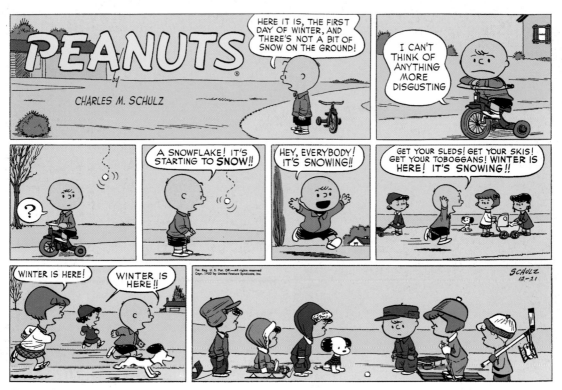

December 21, 1952

January 23, 1955

December 19, 1958

LINUS

Sucking his thumb and gripping his powder-blue blanket, Linus Van Pelt taught us about the meaning of Christmas and convinced us that the Great Pumpkin would bring us presents on Halloween. The deep thinker, he solves problems for all of the PEANUTS gang. His older sister Lucy

"DEAR SANTA, I AM NOT SURE WHAT I WANT FOR CHRISTMAS THIS YEAR. PERHAPS YOU SHOULD SEND ME YOUR CATALOGUE."

can't stand him, but Charlie's little sister Sally is infatuated with him. Despite an ongoing rivalry with Snoopy for the blanket, Linus always comes out on top. He is clearly wise beyond his years.

December 24, 1957

THE '60s

January 6, 1963

December 7, 1960

January 30, 1961

November 16, 1961

December 11, 1961

November 18, 1961

December 7, 1963

December 22, 1963

December 21, 1964

December 22, 1964

PEANUTS THIS IS OUR BIG MOMENT, SNOOPY..

YOU GO OUT ONTO THE STAGE FIRST BECAUSE YOU'RE THE SHEEP...I'LL FOLLOW, AND PRETEND I'M GUIDING YOU...

GO AHEAD..

IF HE EVEN COMES **NEAR** ME WITH THAT SHEPHERD'S STAFF, I'LL GIVE HIM A JUDO CHOP!

12-23

December 23, 1964

PEANUTS "AND THERE WERE IN THE SAME COUNTRY SHEPHERDS ABIDING IN THE FIELD, KEEPING WATCH OVER THEIR FLOCK BY NIGHT."

12-24

PSST! "FLOCK"!

BAAAHH!

December 24, 1964

December 21, 1966

PEPPERMINT PATTY Captain

of her baseball and football teams, Peppermint Patty is a rough-and-tumble girl who would rather be on the playing field than in the classroom. She and her friends Marcie and Franklin attend a different school from Charlie Brown, but they all go to the same summer camp. Throughout the rest of the year, they see each other occasionally—for baseball and football games, as well as at Halloween and Christmas parties.

"DON'T SIGH LIKE THAT MA'AM. . . CHRISTMAS VACATION IS A LONG WAY OFF."

December 22, 1966

PEANUTS 12-24

Tm. Reg. U. S. Pat. Off.—All rights reserved
©1966 by United Feature Syndicate, Inc.

December 24, 1966

December 25, 1966

December 11, 1968

December 26, 1968

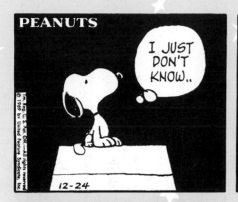

December 24, 1969

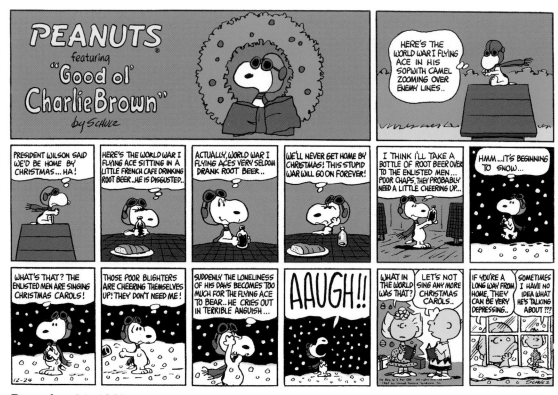

December 24, 1967

December 25, 1969

z

THE '70s

MUSTN'T TOUCH!!

December 26, 1971

December 18, 1972

SALLY

Sally Brown is a silly little sister to Charlie Brown. She spends most of her time making up excuses to stay home from school for a day, coercing her big brother into

"THE STOCKINGS WERE HUNG BY THE CHIMNEY WITH CARE. . IN HOPE THAT JACK NICKLAUS SOON WOULD BE THERE."

doing her homework for her, or pursuing Linus, her unrequited love, her "Sweet Babboo." Easily confused, she once wrote a school report on "Santa Claus and his Rain Gear" and thanked the wrong grandmother for her Christmas presents.

December 22, 1973

December 23, 1973

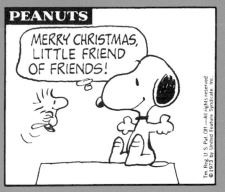

December 25, 1973

December 10, 1976

PEANUTS

A SNOWMAN STANDING ON HIS HEAD!

THAT'S PRETTY GOOD

HE CAN'T DO IT FOR VERY LONG, THOUGH...

ALL THE SNOW RUSHES TO HIS HEAD!

January 6, 1975

December 23, 1979

December 25, 1976

December 24, 1977

January 22, 1978

I'M WRITING A STORY FOR SCHOOL

IT'S ALL ABOUT SANTA CLAUS AND HIS RAIN GEAR

ARE YOU SURE THAT'S RIGHT?

OF COURSE, I'M SURE!

I WONDER IF THAT INCLUDES A FOLDING UMBRELLA..

WHAT'D YOU SAY?

December 18, 1978

THIS IS MY CHRISTMAS STORY..." SANTA AND HIS RAIN GEAR"

"WHEN SANTA LEFT THE NORTH POLE THAT EVENING, A GENTLE MIST WAS FALLING"

"IN HIS YELLOW SLICKER AND BIG RUBBER BOOTS, HE SET OUT ON HIS ANNUAL JOURNEY"

"IT WAS CHRISTMAS EVE, AND SOON CHILDREN AROUND THE WORLD WOULD BE HEARING THE SOUND OF SANTA AND HIS RAIN GEAR"

December 19, 1978

"LITTLE GEORGE WAS WAITING FOR SANTA TO COME"

© 1978 United Feature Syndicate, Inc.

December 20, 1978

"SUDDENLY HE HEARD THE SOUND OF SOMEONE WALKING ON THE ROOF! IT WAS A MAN IN A YELLOW SLICKER AND BIG RUBBER BOOTS!"

12-20

"'I SAW HIM!' SHOUTED LITTLE GEORGE.. 'I SAW SANTA AND HIS RAIN GEAR'"

DON'T SQUIRM, MA'AM, THERE'S MORE TO COME!

SCHULZ

"THE RAIN CAME DOWN HARDER AND HARDER"

© 1978 United Feature Syndicate, Inc.

December 21, 1978

"BUT THE MAN IN THE YELLOW SLICKER AND BIG RUBBER BOOTS NEVER FALTERED"

12-21

"ANOTHER CHRISTMAS EVE HAD PASSED, AND SANTA AND HIS RAIN GEAR HAD DONE THEIR JOB! THE END"

HA HA HA! HA HA! HA HA!

SCHULZ

WOODSTOCK

Whether his hockey team is playing on the birdbath or he's typing letters on Snoopy's behalf, Woodstock is a busy little bird. He speaks only in birdspeak, a complex language of apostrophes and gestures, and he can just as easily express his happiness as his anger. He has been known to give Snoopy birdseed for Christmas and often becomes little more than a mound of snow if he sits still too long in a snowstorm. Above all, he's Snoopy's best friend and has more love and heart than anyone else his size.

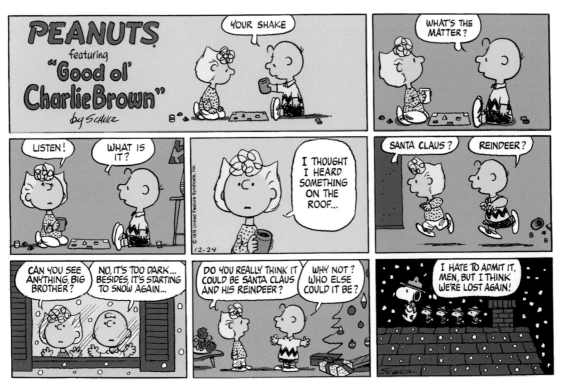

December 24, 1978

THE '80s

I AGREE... ONE OF THE GREAT JOYS IN LIFE IS GOING INTO THE WOODS, AND CUTTING DOWN YOUR OWN CHRISTMAS TREE...

12-17

December 17, 1980

THAT'S TRUE..THERE'S NO SENSE IN CUTTING DOWN THE FIRST ONE YOU SEE...

© 1980 United Feature Syndicate, Inc.

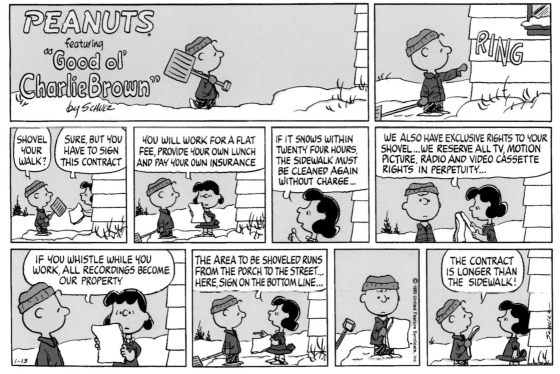

January 13, 1980

LOOK WHAT I GOT YOU FOR CHRISTMAS.. A BOWL FULL OF CHOCOLATE CHIP COOKIES!

WOW!

I JUST HOPE YOU DON'T EAT 'EM ALL AT ONCE..

WHAT DID HE SAY?

12-25

December 25, 1985

December 13, 1980

SCHROEDER

A prodigy with a toy piano, Schroeder idolizes Beethoven and cannot be bothered with much else. Much of his Christmas season is spent avoiding Lucy and mistletoe; he much prefers his favorite holiday, Beethoven's birthday. He can

"I'VE BEEN READING UP ON WINTER."

always be counted on for his musical talents, however, and is always a part of any school production.

December 18, 1981

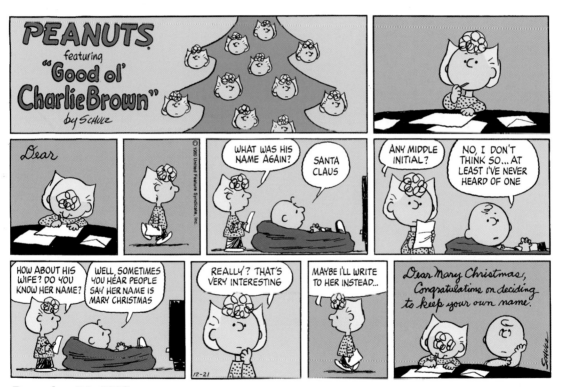

December 21, 1980

December 26, 1982

December 10, 1984

December 19, 1983

December 25, 1983

December 20, 1981

SNOOPY

Snoopy does it all—he's everything from a World War I Flying Ace to an accomplished writer to a tennis champion to a trickster. He has a weakness for root beer and pizza, often consuming so much that he spends the night atop his doghouse listening to his stomach rumble. He is protective of his best friend, Woodstock, and the two make sure to exchange Christmas presents every year. Snoopy is a true Renaissance beagle.

"ANYONE WHO WOULD FLY AROUND FROM HOUSE TO HOUSE IN A SLEIGH WITH A BUNCH OF REINDEER HAS TO BE OUT OF HIS MIND!"

December 7, 1985

December 21, 1989

November 15, 1987

Dear Santa Claus, I hope this letter reaches you before Christmas.

12-13 © 1986 United Feature Syndicate, Inc.

I am worried about something.

When you come to fill my stocking...

Please be careful. Love, Spike

December 13, 1986

MARCIE

The complete opposite of her best friend, Peppermint Patty, Marcie has both book smarts and common sense—but she is completely inept at sports. She insists on calling Peppermint Patty "Sir" in the face of all Patty's protests and is always nearby if Peppermint Patty's around. Even though she's not confident on the baseball diamond, she always participates and finds areas in which she can excel; she was Mary in the Christmas pageant.

"MY FAMILY SAID IT'S ALL RIGHT TO BELIEVE IN SANTA CLAUS, BUT NOT THE GREAT PUMPKIN."

December 25, 1988

December 20, 1989

December 19, 1989

December 19, 1986

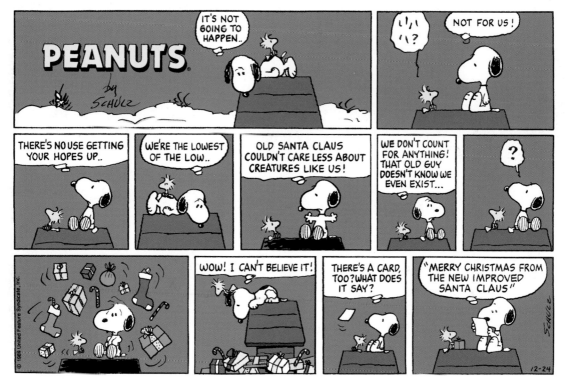

December 24, 1989

PSST, BIG BROTHER ..I HATE TO WAKE YOU ON CHRISTMAS EVE, BUT I NEED YOUR ADVICE...

© 1985 United Feature Syndicate,Inc. 12-24

I WAS SOUND ASLEEP WHEN ALL OF A SUDDEN VISIONS OF SUGARPLUMS DANCED IN MY HEAD!

WHAT ARE SUGAR-PLUMS?

THEY'RE SORT OF ROUND PIECES OF CANDY...

GOOD! I WAS AFRAID I WAS FREAKING OUT!

December 24, 1985

December 22, 1989

THE '90s

November 29, 1995

November 30, 1995

December 1, 1995

December 2, 1995

December 12, 1998

December 22, 1996

December 26, 1991

December 21, 1990

FRANKLIN

In 1968, Charlie Brown made a new friend at the beach. Franklin goes to a different school in town, where he is good friends with Peppermint Patty and Marcie. He plays against Charlie Brown on Peppermint Patty's baseball team, but the rivalry doesn't get in the way of their friendship— he is always invited to the Christmas party. During the year, Franklin goes to the movies with the rest of the PEANUTS gang and he and Charlie Brown have long talks about their grampas.

November 17, 1990

December 25, 1990

December 23, 1990

December 24, 1990

SPIKE

Snoopy and his brother Spike were separated as puppies at the Daisy Hill Puppy Farm. While Snoopy took the traditional path after graduation and went to live with Charlie Brown, Spike moved to the desert, where he gets along on his

"ONE OF THE GREAT JOYS OF LIFE IS SITTING BY YOUR CHRISTMAS TREE WHILE BIG FLUFFY SNOWFLAKES FLOAT GENTLY TO THE GROUND . . . OR A NICE SANDSTORM."

own with the company of "Joe Cactus" and several friendly tumbleweeds. Spike always celebrates Christmas, despite the distinct lack of snow in the desert and he and Snoopy exchange Christmas cards annually.

December 24, 1995

I THOUGHT MAYBE I'D GET A DOG FOR CHRISTMAS, BUT I DIDN'T..

January 2, 1996

OWNING A DOG IS A BIG RESPONSIBILITY, RERUN..THEY NEED LOTS OF CARE..

© 1995 United Feature Syndicate, Inc.

AND THEY NEED A LOT OF COMFORTING..

1-2-96

December 1, 1997

November 27, 1992

November 21, 1990

December 25, 1994

November 28, 1995

December 8, 1998

Charles Schulz (1922–2000)

"Someday, Charles, you're going to be an artist," his kindergarten teacher once told him. She probably didn't know how prophetic those words would be, but Charles "Sparky" Schulz grew up to become one of the most recognized names in comics.

Born to a barber in Minnesota, Charles Schulz grew up with dreams of writing his own comic strip. After admirable service in World War II, he returned to his passion, drawing, and he took a position as a teacher with his alma mater, Art Instruction Schools. While there, Schulz further honed his skills and met many of the people who would inspire his future work (including a friend named Charlie Brown and a girl with red hair who broke his heart).

Soon he was creating his own comic, which he called "L'il Folks" (it featured a younger Charlie Brown). The *Saturday Evening Post* printed several single comic panels, and the *St. Paul Pioneer Press* made it a weekly feature. "L'il Folks" became the focus of Schulz's career. After expanding it from a single panel to a strip format, he signed a five-year contract with United Feature Syndicate and began his lifelong dream: he was a full-time cartoonist. Because of legal issues surrounding the name "L'il Folks"—"Little Folks" and "L'il Abner" already existed—the strip was renamed PEANUTS, much to Schulz's displeasure.

Over the next fifty years, the world grew to love Charlie Brown, Snoopy, Linus and even Lucy. PEANUTS fans know the characters as well as they know their families, sharing in their losses as well as their triumphs. Every time Charlie Brown missed the football (thanks to Lucy's shenanigans), we missed it, too. When Linus awaited the arrival of the Great Pumpkin, we were out there in the pumpkin patch with him. As Snoopy flew through the air fighting The Red Baron, we flew right alongside him. By mixing humor, friendship, love and life, Charles Schulz made PEANUTS one of the longest-running, most popular comics of all time—and no one but Schulz himself ever drew a panel.

PEANUTS remained Schulz's focus throughout his life, and it became the most popular comic strip ever. It has been published in 21 languages, *in* more than 2,600 newspapers, and has spawned dozens of books, over 50 television specials and even a Broadway musical. *The Joy of a Peanuts Christmas* is Schulz's classic collection of holiday strips, a tribute Hallmark is proud to sponsor.

Charles Schulz died on February 12, 2000, in Santa Rosa, California at the age of 77—only hours before his last original PEANUTS strip was scheduled to appear in Sunday newspapers.